Mermaid KINGDOM

D0526172

30131 05347730 0

LONDON BOROUGH OF BARNET

Raintree is an imprint of Capstone Global Library
Limited, a company incorporated in England and Wales
having its registered office at 7 Pilgrim Street, London,
EC4V 6LB – Registered company number: 6695582

www.raintree.co.uk
myorders@raintree.co.uk

Copyright © Capstone Global Library Limited 2015
The moral rights of the proprietor have been asserted.

All rights reserved. No part of this publication may be
reproduced in any form or by any means (including
photocopying or storing it in any medium by electronic
means and whether or not transiently or incidentally
to some other use of this publication) without the
written permission of the copyright owner, except in
accordance with the provisions of the Copyright, Designs
and Patents Act 1988 or under the terms of a licence
issued by the Copyright Licensing Agency, Saffron
House, 6–10 Kirby Street, London EC1N 8TS (www.cla.
co.uk). Applications for the copyright owner's written
permission should be addressed to the publisher.

Designed by Alison Thiele

Artistic Elements: Shutterstock

ISBN 978 1 4062 9294 7 (paperback)
18 17 16 15 14
10 9 8 7 6 5 4 3 2 1

British Library Cataloguing in Publication Data
A full catalogue record for this book is available from
the British Library.

Printed and bound in China.

Rachel's Secret

by Janet Gurtler

illustrated by Katie Wood

raintree 🍃

a Capstone company — publishers for children

Mermaid life

⭐ Mermaid Kingdom refers to all the kingdoms in the sea, including Neptunia, Caspian, Hercules, Titania and Nessland. Each kingdom has a King and Queen who live in a castle. Merpeople live in caves.

⭐ Mermaids get their legs on their thirteenth birthdays at the stroke of midnight. It's a celebration when the mermaid makes her first voyage onto land. After their thirteenth birthdays, mermaids can go onto land for short periods of time but must be very careful.

⭐ If a mermaid goes onto land before her thirteenth birthday, she will get her legs early and never get her tail back. She will lose all memories of being a mermaid and will be human forever.

⭐ Mermaids are able to stay on land with legs for no more than forty-eight hours. Any longer and they will not be able to get their tails back and will be human forever. They will lose all memories of being a mermaid.

⭐ If they fall in love, merpeople and humans can marry and have babies (with special permission from the King and Queen of their kingdom). Their babies are half-human and half-merperson. However, this love must be the strongest love possible in order for it to be approved by the King and Queen.

⭐ Half-human mermaids are able to go on land indefinitely and can change back into a mermaid at any point. However, they are not allowed to tell other humans about the mermaid world unless they have special permission from the King and Queen.

Chapter one

Shyanna and Cora were chasing each other around, laughing so much that tears were falling down their rosy cheeks.

"Come on, Rachel!" Shyanna shouted to me.

My friends flipped in circles, swishing their glorious sparkling mermaid tails behind them. I smiled from the swing where I sat watching them, loving my two new friends with all my heart.

"Remember when, at your twelfth birthday party, you tried to convince Alexa you were thirteen?" Cora asked Shyanna. She looked at me and explained, "Alexa almost ended up getting beached in an effort to see Shyanna's legs."

"Oh, I still feel terrible about that," Shyanna said.

"Only because you got into so much trouble!" Cora added.

They both giggled, and I had to admit that a small part of me felt left out. I was new to Neptunia. After my mum had died, our entire life changed. My dad and I needed to start again, and moving to Neptunia was just what we needed. We've just moved here.

I was lucky to have two best friends already, but it didn't make everything perfect. I missed my old best friend, Owen, every day. Sometimes I even missed living in Caspian and being closer to land. It was easier to get to the beach and meet up with Owen from there.

Yes, Owen was a human. And having a human as a best friend had its challenges, especially because he didn't know that I'm a mermaid. Confused yet?

Here's some background: My mum was human before she became a mermaid. My dad fell in love with her when he had spent some time on land. Because their love was so strong, she was given special permission from the King and Queen to become a mermaid and marry him. I was half-human. I could go on land whenever I wanted for as long as I wanted. It really was an incredible love story.

Shyanna was the only one who knew my big secret, and I intended to keep it that way. It was hard enough being the new mermaid in Neptunia. I couldn't imagine how the other mermaids would feel if they knew I was half-human!

"I can't wait for my real thirteenth birthday," Shyanna said as she twirled around. "I can't wait to get my legs! My leg ceremony is going to be so wonderful!" Her eyes opened wider, and she glanced at me. "I mean, the ceremony is only part of it. Having legs and being able to walk on land will be the best part."

I knew she was trying to make me feel better.
I wouldn't have a legs ceremony on my thirteenth
birthday. Because I was half-human, I already had
my legs. I could go on land whenever I wanted for
as long as I wanted. No matter what, I'd always be a
little bit different. I knew it was okay to be different,
but that didn't make it easy.

I didn't even bother to tell Cora and Shyanna that
my thirteenth birthday was the next day. It wasn't the
big day it would have been if I was a real mermaid,
so I didn't want them to know.

Cora swam over to the swings and floated around
me. "Hey, you! There's no need to look unhappy when
you could be playing tag with us!" Cora squealed.
She grabbed my arm and playfully pulled me off the
swing. "Come on, I need your help! Shyanna goes a
bit mad when we play tag."

I couldn't help laughing and chased after
Shyanna with her. It was hard to stay miserable for
long with my two new friends. I raced after Shyanna,

but Cora ended up catching her first. Cora was the fastest swimmer I'd ever seen!

We were still laughing when a royal trumpeter and messenger swam into Walrus Waterpark. We immediately stopped and floated to attention. The trumpet player lifted his trumpet to play the royal fanfare. A purple royal flag dangled from the middle of the trumpet as he played the royal tune.

When he had finished, the messenger unrolled a scroll, cleared her throat and began to read. "The Queen would like to invite Rachel Marlin, Cora Bass and Shyanna Angler to appear with her in a Royal Concert," she announced. "Queen Kenna has requested you sing as her opening act a week from today in the Royal Gardens."

"Of course!" we all squealed in delight. That was an incredible honour! Our show-stopping performance at the Melody Carnival had clearly not gone unnoticed by the Queen.

One of the reasons my dad and I had just

moved to Neptunia was so that he could be the Queen's singing teacher. That's how I met Shyanna and Cora. It's a long story, but I basically saved Shyanna, then she saved me, and then all three of us ended up singing together and becoming best friends. I suppose it's not a really long story after all!

"Wow!" Cora said. "I never thought I'd be invited to sing with the Queen!"

"It must be because of the Melody Carnival," I said. "She told my dad how impressed she'd been with us!"

Shyanna and Cora swam in little circles and shrieked with excitement again. Their energy was definitely contagious.

"My dad hinted that she might have a concert," I confided to them. "She's improved so much, and I think she wants to show off a bit."

I hated to boast, but my dad really was the best singing teacher in all of the Mermaid Kingdoms.

"I have to go home to tell my sisters," Cora said. "They'll be thrilled – and jealous!"

"I need to tell my mum!" Shyanna said.

My dad already knew, and the only other person I wanted to tell was Owen. But I couldn't do that, of course. He didn't even know I was a mermaid. I wished so much that I could share my secret with him, but that wasn't possible, no matter how hard I wished for it.

Chapter two

When I woke up the next day, my dad was already at work. I was a bit disappointed that he had already gone. It was my birthday, and I was all alone. However, he did leave me a nice note telling me to get ready for our fun day together. He was going to be home after lunch.

Dad and I had planned a father-daughter day. We were going to spend our time exploring the sea. He'd been so busy since we'd moved to Neptunia. The Queen and her royal mermaids were all having singing lessons, which took up a lot of time. We'd hardly had any time together.

I spent the morning plaiting and beading my hair and polishing my tail. I was so excited about our day together that I was waiting at the door for Dad to come home. But as soon as he swam inside, I could tell our plans would have to change.

He pulled a bouquet of flowers out from behind his back. "Happy birthday, Rachel. I hate to do this, but our plans will have to change. I'll be home a little bit late, but we'll celebrate then. I promise I'll make it up to you." He could tell I was disappointed.

"That's fine," I said, but I didn't mean it.

"I'm really sorry, sweetheart," he said. "The Queen requested an extra rehearsal this afternoon, and I couldn't get out of it."

"Thanks, Dad," I said. I was trying really hard not to cry.

"I wish we had organized a party. You are thirteen, after all," he said, frowning.

"No," I said. "I didn't want to make a fuss about it."

He kissed my forehead. "You're just like your mother. She never wanted to have parties for herself either. Could you at least go and see Shyanna and Cora? I'll be home with cake later. I'm so sorry."

"It's okay," I told him. "It's not your fault. You work for the Queen. We knew you'd be busy!"

He rushed back to work, and I called Shyanna. Her mum said she and Cora were at the waterpark with Cora's sister, so I swam over there. When I arrived, I saw them pushing Cora's littlest sister on the swings.

"Wow!" Shyanna said when she spotted me. "You look amazing! What's the occasion?"

"Not much," I said. "I was supposed to be going out with my dad, but he's busy with the Queen for the rest of the day."

"Aww," Shyanna said. "That's a shame. I bet you were really looking forward to it."

She swam over to touch my hair. "How did you do that to your hair? It's so pretty."

"It looks incredible!" Cora agreed, and she swam over to have a look at my red plaits.

"Cora, you should wear yours like that for your thirteenth birthday!" Shyanna said.

"Great idea." The girls fussed over my hair and admired the sparkles and glitter I'd added to my tail. But soon baby Jewel started to cry, so my friends swam back to the swings and started pushing again.

"I can't wait for my leg ceremony!" Cora said. "Mainly so that I can go onto land and get some peace and quiet for a few hours."

I smiled at her. Her life was so different from mine. She was always so busy looking after her sisters or helping her mum around the house. She hardly ever had any time to herself, which was something I had plenty of!

"I can't wait to have cake!" Shyanna shouted. "With oyster icing!"

Cora laughed. "You're always after cake."

"Yes. And today is Friday. We should have cake!" Shyanna joked.

I smiled, but then it clicked. Friday!

When I lived in Caspian, Friday was the day I'd always gone to visit Owen. Now I realized I had the perfect opportunity. Who better to see on my birthday now that dad was busy with the Queen? It took longer to swim to shore to see Owen now that I lived in Neptunia, but I had extra time.

"Um ... I have to get going," I said and somersaulted in delight.

"Where are you going?" Cora asked.

"Just back to my cave to relax," I said. I hated to lie to Cora, but I couldn't tell her the truth.

Shyanna and I exchanged a knowing look. I waved and smiled at them as I swam as fast as I could out of the waterpark. The sooner I could get to Owen, the better!

Chapter three

I stumbled on the rocks and raced up the beach.
My legs always felt a little wobbly and unsteady when
they first changed from my tail into legs. I coughed,
getting used to breathing in fresh air instead of
filtering sea water through my gills.

I was at the spot where I'd first met Owen. This
was also the same place where Shyanna almost got
her legs too early when she went searching for throat
medication. This was the spot where I saved her and
our friendship was established. This was truly one

of the best spots in the world. So many incredible memories were made here.

"Hey, clumsy!" a voice yelled.

"Owen!" I jumped up and down, waving. I ran towards him, and even though I'm not a great runner, I managed to get to his side quickly. I stopped, suddenly a little shy. "It's so good to see you."

"I had a feeling you were finally going to show up!" Owen said. "It's Friday! You always used to show up on Fridays." He stared at me for a second. "You look really nice."

"Thanks," I said. "And sorry I haven't been here for a while. I've had trouble getting away."

Since my mum had died and we had moved to Neptunia, it was a lot harder to see Owen. He didn't know why I couldn't see him as much, but he didn't question it. He was a good friend.

"Well, I'm glad you're back," he said. "Especially as it's your birthday!" He grinned and then started walking, gesturing for me to follow.

"You remembered?" I couldn't wipe the smile off my face as I scrambled to follow him.

"Of course I remembered!" he said, turning to me with his familiar sparkling grin. "Come on!"

"Where are we going?" I asked.

"My house," he said. "I had a feeling you'd show up, and I asked my mum to make you a cake. Just in case. Don't tell everyone, but I think you're secretly her favourite friend of mine."

"She made me a cake?" That made me so happy I almost cried. As we walked, I made a promise to myself to see Owen every Friday from now on. No more excuses.

"My mum loves you, and she loves making cakes," Owen told me. "It was a win-win situation."

"She is the best!" I said.

"Justin, Mitchel and Morgan are on their way over," Owen said. "They're having their swimming lesson, but when they heard my mum was making a cake, I couldn't stop them!"

His other friends were always nice to me too. It made me wonder why some mermaids are afraid of humans.

When we got to his house, his mum said, "Rachel! You're here!" Then she went into the kitchen and brought out the cake she had made.

She'd decorated the cake like a beautiful red-headed mermaid. My eyes bulged out of my head.

She laughed. "Don't you like it? I'm sorry. I only have boys. I assumed all girls loved mermaids as much as I do! I've always wished they were real."

"Me too," I told her with a big grin. "I love it!"

The three boys barged in the front door then, just in time for cake.

Owen's mum put candles on the cake, lit them with a match, and they all sang "Happy Birthday" to me. We each stuffed ourselves with cake, and then Owen stood up and left the kitchen. He came back holding a pretty pink gift bag and put it on the table in front of me.

"A present? Is Rachel your girlfriend?" Morgan teased, grinning.

Owen's face turned red, and I felt my face get hot. I avoided looking at him when I reached inside the bag. I took out a box. Inside was a beautiful shell necklace.

"Do you like it?" Owen asked. "I can take it back if you don't. Mum helped me choose it."

"It's perfect!" I said and immediately put it on. I decided I might never take it off.

His friends made embarrassing whistles and kissy noises.

"We're just friends," Owen said. He looked so sweet when he blushed. Not in a boyfriend way, either. He will always just be my best friend, which was exactly what I wanted.

I wished I could stay longer, but I knew I should get back to Neptunia. I reluctantly thanked Owen's mum for the cake. "I have to get going. My dad will expect me home soon," I said.

"I'll walk you back to the beach," Owen offered.

He thought I lived in a house nearby, and he never went further than the edge of the beach with me. I had made it seem as though my dad was really strict, because that seemed like the easiest excuse. I'd wait an extra five minutes to make sure Owen was gone, and then I'd slip back into the water and return to life in the sea. Thankfully Owen wasn't nosey, or my secret would have crumbled around me.

"I wish you could come out more," Owen said when we reached the edge of the beach. His cheeks were a little bit red again. "Why don't you come out as much as you used to?"

I stared at my feet. "I wish I could tell you," I whispered. "But you wouldn't understand."

I couldn't tell Owen I was a mermaid – or even half a mermaid. The secret was protected by mermaid magic. If I told him without special permission from the Queen or King, I'd never get my tail back and I'd have to live as a human forever.

After a few months without my tail, I'd forget that I'd ever been a mermaid at all. I knew the rules.

"Is everything okay?" Owen asked.

"Everything is fine! I promise," I told him. "I have a couple of new mer ... friends. And they're really nice. I'm busy. But I miss you too." Owen knew I'd had a difficult year, but he didn't know I'd moved to a new Mermaid Kingdom. Obviously.

"Are you sure?" he asked.

"Everything is fine, I promise," I said.

"Okay," he said. "But remember ... there's nothing you could tell me that would make me not want to be your friend."

I smiled. "Thanks, Owen," I said.

"Will you be back next Friday?" he asked. "I'm having a party at my house."

"It's your thirteenth birthday," I said, suddenly remembering.

But then I remembered that Friday was the concert too.

He looked at my face. "What's wrong?"

I dropped my gaze to my toes. "I can't believe it," I said. "I'm in a concert that night. Singing for the Queen – uh, I mean, someone really important. I've promised to do it. I'm so sorry." Telling Owen I couldn't go to his party felt worse than stepping on a stingray.

Owen dropped his head. "No. It's okay," he said, but he couldn't hide his disappointment.

There was no way to get out of singing, but there was also no way I could miss Owen's birthday party. Especially when he went out of his way to make mine so special!

"I'll try to think of something," I said.

What was I going to do?

Chapter four

I swam quickly through the sea, and even though I felt sad about Owen's party, I couldn't help smiling at a group of lobsters and crabs who waved at me along the way. I really did love all the creatures in the sea, and they helped to cheer me up.

The guards outside Neptunia nodded when I swam through the coral entrance. They were getting used to my coming and going.

When I darted inside the front door at home, Dad was sitting at the kitchen table.

"Rachel," he said. "Where were you?"

"Hi, Dad," I said. "I went to see Owen. I miss him more than I thought I would."

"I thought as much," he said. "But from now on, you need to let me know. I was getting worried."

"Sorry, Dad," I replied.

That's when I noticed a big cake sitting on the middle of the table. Thirteen unlit candles were stuck on top.

"I feel terrible for messing up your birthday," he said. "I should have planned a party and had your friends over. I'm not as good at these things as your mum was."

"Well, I spent the day with my best friend, which made it really special. Owen couldn't have come for a party anyway," I reminded him.

"I suppose so." He patted my hand when I sat down next to him. "The Queen's chef made the cake when I told her it was your birthday. It's your favourite – shrimp-vanilla."

I didn't tell him that Owen's mum had made a cake too. And that it had been one of the most delicious cakes I'd ever tasted.

He put his arm around me. "I'm sorry we didn't have a birthday party for you."

"It's okay, Dad. I had a great birthday. And I'd love a slice of cake," I said. Then I forced myself to eat a big slice even though I was already full.

* * *

The week flew by with lots of rehearsals and fun. Finally the night of the concert arrived. I was so excited about singing, but I couldn't stop thinking about Owen and his party.

Shyanna had invited Cora and me to her house on Friday afternoon. Shyanna's mum made us some snacks while we got ready. I'd offered to help Shyanna plait her hair. She stared at my necklace as I plaited the front of her hair.

"Oh! That's beautiful. Is it new? Where did you get it?" Shyanna asked.

"Um ... I got it from a friend," I said, and glanced at Cora.

Cora's hair was curled in beautiful waves, and she was glossing up her purple tail with fish oil. She wasn't paying attention to us.

"An old friend," I added quietly.

Shyanna's eyes nearly popped out of her head. "Owen?" she whispered, but she wasn't quiet enough.

Cora swam closer and stuck her face right up to mine. "Who's Owen? Is he your boyfriend?"

"No," I said, but my cheeks reddened like a lobster in boiling water. "I mean, he's a boy, and he's a friend. But he's not a boyfriend."

"Why did he buy you a necklace, then?" Cora asked, putting her hands on her hips.

"It was for my birthday," I said quietly. I moved behind Shyanna to admire my work.

Shyanna spun around. "Your birthday? When is your birthday?"

"It was last Friday," I admitted and patted her plaits. "I've finished your hair," I told her. "It looks beautiful. It's your best look yet."

"It's just been your birthday and you didn't tell us?" Shyanna said. She looked surprised, cross, hurt and sad all at the same time. She knew my secret, so I was surprised by her reaction.

Cora flipped in semicircles. "Your thirteenth birthday? You had a leg ceremony without us?" Her mouth hung open, and she looked hurt too.

Shyanna and I exchanged a look. "We'll make it up to her later," Shyanna said with fake enthusiasm. "Right now, we should rehearse our song!" She was trying to distract Cora. She belted out the first line of the song. I joined in, thankful when Cora stopped frowning and sang along with us.

"We're all ready to go!" Shyanna announced when we had finished the song. She hurried us off to have something to eat, and luckily, kept up the conversation about things other than my birthday until we left for the big concert.

When we arrived at the Royal Gardens, we all took a deep breath. It was transformed with a stage that looked like the inside of an oyster shell. Shiny shells and pearls were strung together and hung from a peach coral reef dripping with sea flowers. It was beautiful!

Other mermaids who'd been picked to sing with the Queen were fussing behind the stage. Stage-hands roamed around them, some carrying huge stage props. Somehow I'd become separated from Cora and Shyanna and was shoved into a tight space with a group of other mergirls from Neptunia. I recognized one mermaid whose name was Regina. Shyanna had said she was the most popular girl in the school.

Regina noticed me straight away. "You're Mr Marlin's daughter, aren't you? The Queen's new singing teacher?"

I nodded.

"I saw you sing in the twelve-year-old category at the Melody Carnival. You were really good," said one of the other mermaids.

"Thanks," I said and smiled at her.

Regina glared back at me. "When are you thirteen?" she asked, putting her hands on her hips.

"Um. I already am." I said, wondering why she seemed so cross with me. "My birthday was last Friday."

"But you didn't have a party!" said Regina. "At least I didn't hear about it. And I hear about all the important parties in Neptunia."

"I had a party," I said straight away. "It just wasn't in Neptunia."

"But how could you have your leg ceremony without Shyanna and Cora?" Regina asked. "I saw them at Walrus Waterpark last Friday. I thought they were your best friends. That seems ... fishy."

My cheeks burned. I couldn't think of anything to say. I glanced around, wishing the stage-hands would hurry up so I could get away. I wished Shyanna and Cora would appear to defend me and get Regina to go away. She was acting as if I'd done

something wrong. I didn't even know her! I didn't know what was wrong with her.

Then Regina narrowed her eyes. "You know ... my mum heard a rumour. A rumour about your mum," she said with a smug look on her face.

I sucked in a deep breath. Oh no. Was she going to start teasing me because my mum was human and I was half-human? Some mermaids didn't approve of humans who became a mermaid by magic.

"My mum was amazing," I said, swallowing a lump in my throat.

"Regina," the nice mermaid said. "Her mum is dead. Don't be nasty."

Regina wrinkled up her nose and moved away from me as if I smelled like three-day-old fish fries. "I only hope the rumours about your mum aren't true." And with that, she turned her back on me.

The nice mermaid smiled weakly at me, but turned back to the group. "Remember my leg ceremony? Everyone said it was the best one ever!"

Regina said to her friends as she flipped her hair and batted her long eyelashes.

The other mermaids looked guilty, but they nodded. Finally the stage-hands cleared out of the way, and the group swam off, Regina at the front.

Just then, Shyanna and Cora swam over.

"There you are!" Shyanna cried. "We've been looking everywhere for you. We're on in five minutes! Can you believe it?"

"Are you okay?" Cora asked, looking at me more closely.

"I'm fine." I faked a smile.

"I saw Regina," Cora said. "Was she being horrible?"

"No, I'm fine," I tried to reassure them.

They looked like they didn't believe me, but it was too complicated to explain because Cora didn't know the truth yet. I knew I had to tell her soon, but I was waiting for the right moment.

An usher came along and hurried us to the stage,

and then, before I knew it, we were performing our song. It sounded really fantastic. I felt like I was in a dream the whole time we were singing. And before I knew it, it was over.

It went by so quickly! All of our hard work and all of our rehearsing had paid off. It was amazing how much music could still make me feel better.

After we had finished, Cora and Shyanna hurried out into the audience to watch the rest of the show and to look after Cora's sisters.

"Do you want to come along?" Cora asked.

I shook my head. "I'm going to stay here in case my dad needs help."

That was partly true. But I also had a plan.

Regina swam by to go on stage and looked straight at me. "She's not even a real mermaid," she whispered to a friend, and both girls turned away from me.

I glanced at my dad behind the curtains. He was so happy directing the show and was completely in his element. I looked at my phone.

I wanted to see Owen so badly! If I left straight away, I could get to his party and be back before anyone missed me.

My dad had told me a hundred times that I needed to tell him when I was going to go onto land, but he was too busy to bother right then. Plus, he didn't even have to know. I would be back before he even noticed I was gone.

I swam out of the Royal Gardens, and then out of the kingdom and towards the beach. When I got to land and grew legs, I hurried up the beach towards Owen's house.

Before I even reached Owen's front gate, I could hear the party. Owen's house was lit up with glowing party lights. Happy noises floated through the air. I walked up the path towards the house and was about to ring the doorbell to join the party when I heard noises and shouts.

"Last one in is a rotten egg!" someone shouted.

The thundering army of friends sounded louder

than a sea storm. Everyone was running out through the garden towards the beach, all of them in their swimming shorts. Owen led the pack, laughing, with Justin, Morgan and Mitchel at his side as they raced to the water. My heart sank. I went to watch them, knowing I couldn't go and see Owen now. Being so close to water was too risky. If I got any salt water on me, my tail would reappear.

Instead, I went as close to the shore as I could and watched from the shadows.

Owen and his friends were having so much fun. Owen looked so happy. He didn't look like he missed me at all.

I went back to his house to leave him his present. I'd plaited seaweed into a necklace and attached a real shark's tooth. I left his present at the front door and then walked off down the road to a quiet beach. I leapt back into the water, feeling like I didn't belong in either one of my worlds.

Chapter five

In the morning, I was so tired from all my sneaking about. Dad had to go and see the Queen early to review her performances, and he'd told me to have a lie-in. I stayed in bed all morning, but before lunch, the doorbell started ringing and didn't stop.

"Rachel, I know you're in there," a voice shouted from outside. "Let me in, lazy bones!"

With a big sigh, I got up and swam to the front door. When I opened it, my jaw dropped.

Shyanna floated on the front porch, holding a giant bouquet of balloons shaped like sea creatures in one hand and a starfish-shaped gift bag in the other hand.

"Happy belated birthday, sleepyhead!" she cried. "Cora and I got these for you. She wanted to come too, but her sisters are poorly and her mum wouldn't let her leave."

My heart filled with happiness. "You look like a one-mermaid party pack!"

Shyanna laughed. "Are you going to let me in?'

"Oh!" I opened the door, and she handed me the balloons and the present as we went inside. "Thank you so much!" I said. I tied the balloons to a chair in the living room and put the present down on the table.

"I still can't believe we missed your birthday!" Shyanna said.

"It's okay. I mean, turning thirteen is not as big a deal for me, because I already have legs." I sat in the chair with the balloons and grinned. Shyanna sat opposite me.

"Still ... it was your birthday! Everyone deserves to feel extra special on their birthday," she said, making a really good point.

"I went to see Owen," I told her. "His mum made me a cake. And his friends came over."

Shyanna clapped her hands together. "I'm glad. He seems like a good friend. I wish I could have come! Will you introduce me to Owen when I get my legs? I've never met a human before!"

Before I could answer, the doorbell rang. I got up and floated over to the door. When I opened it, Cora was flipping around in circles. She tackled me immediately, hugging me and giggling. "My mum let me come. My sisters are all sleeping!"

Cora swam inside and pulled me along behind her. "Hooray!" she said when she saw the table. "You haven't opened your present yet. Open it now!" she cried.

The girls spun around while I opened the bag and pulled out matching bracelets made of black pearls and plaited seaweed. "One for each of us!" Cora said. "Friendship bracelets for forever friends!"

We all slipped them onto our wrists and held them out to admire them.

"They're beautiful," I said. "Thank you."

"So," Cora said. "I've been dying to know. Who's this Owen that you're so close to? You didn't think I would forget to ask you about him, did you?"

I glanced at Shyanna and then swam closer to Cora and took her hand. "I have a secret," I said. "Shyanna already knows because she caught me in the act, but I made her promise not to tell anyone."

Cora looked at me and then at Shyanna and then back at me, blinking. Waiting.

"I'm sorry I didn't tell you earlier. It's hard. I get teased," I said. "And I loved my mum so much, it's hard to talk about it."

Cora grabbed my other hand. "What? What's wrong, Rachel?" Cora asked.

I took a deep breath and closed my eyes. "My mum was a human."

I waited for her to drop my hand or pull away in disgust or something.

"So?" she said.

I opened my eyes and started to laugh. "That's all you have to say? It means I'm half-human."

She let go of my hands. "Oh. That doesn't matter at all." She opened her eyes wide and her mouth wider. "Wait. Does that mean you have legs? And that you can use them whenever you like?"

I nodded, and she stared at me without even blinking. "That is amazing," she said, in total awe. "It must be a romantic story, your mum and dad. Wouldn't it be amazing to fall in love with a human? How magical."

Shyanna cleared her throat, raised her eyebrows, and stared at me. I knew she was thinking about me and Owen.

"Stop looking at me like that, Shy. Owen and I are not in love," I told her. "We are just friends. Best friends – nothing more."

Cora looked backwards and forwards between Shyanna and me. "Wait. What? Is this boyfriend of yours a human?" she asked me.

I touched the shell necklace Owen had given me. "A friend who's a boy. And yes. Owen is human. And he doesn't know I'm a mermaid."

"Wow!" Cora went to the table and sat opposite Shyanna. "How did you meet a human?" They both stared at me, waiting for more information, I suppose.

"Some of the mermaids from Caspian found out I was half-human, and they used to tease me. I went to land a lot to escape, and that's when I met Owen. At first, I was a bit scared of him, but he's so nice and adventurous. We quickly became best friends. I didn't have to worry about getting teased when I was with him. I used to visit him at least once a week, but I haven't been visiting as much since we moved to Neptunia."

"What's it like? To have a human as a friend?" Cora asked.

"He's great," I said. "He makes me feel important. I mean, he's like us. Only he isn't able to enjoy the sea like we can. That does make me feel sad."

Shyanna and Cora nodded. I could tell they were both thinking how awful it would be not be able to enjoy the sea like we were able to.

"The thing is, I've been away so much," I said. "I'm worried he's going to forget about me."

"He won't forget about you," Shyanna said, and Cora nodded in agreement.

"How could he?" Cora said.

"Thanks," I said, smiling and looking down at my friendship bracelet. "I got teased a lot in Caspian. The other mermaids were really nasty. And Owen was so important to me. He still is. And the thing is, I think my secret is out again. I think one of the mermaids here knows about my mum."

"Who cares? The mermaids here won't tease you," Shyanna said confidently.

"I don't know," I said doubtfully. "The mermaid who hinted about it ... she didn't seem happy at all.

I don't want everyone to think of me as being different. I hate being different."

"Who was it?" Cora asked, jumping up again. She found it difficult to stay still.

"Regina," I said quietly.

"Regina Merrick? She can be really nasty," Shyanna said. "Was she being nasty to you?"

Cora was pace-swimming around the room. I shrugged and looked away. "It doesn't matter. I'm tired of having to keep secrets from everyone," I said. "I hate hiding the fact that I'm a mermaid from Owen. It is awful. He is my best friend, and he has no idea what my real life is like."

"You're perfect," Cora said. "Just the way you are."

"I don't feel like it." I paused before I made my big announcement. The thing I'd been thinking about all night. "But I think I have a solution," I told them.

They both stared at me, waiting.

I stared back. Then, slowly, I said, "I think I might want to become human. Permanently."

Chapter six

Silence.

Complete silence. That's the response I got to my big announcement.

"I've thought about it a lot," I said, slowly swimming towards the table. "It's not an easy decision to make."

Shyanna and Cora both looked shell-shocked.

"Why would you want to do that?" Cora asked quietly, frowning.

"It just seems easier," I said.

I slumped down in my chair, and we all faced each other in a circle. "You know how mermaid magic works," I said. "I would stay on land and not go near salt water for six months. After that, I would lose my tail. I could swim in the sea, and it still wouldn't come back. And after I lost my tail, I would slowly start to forget that I'd ever been a mermaid. I would have memories of my life, of course, but it would all be very hazy. I'd believe I had always been human. End of story."

"You'd be willing to do that for a boy?" Cora asked, shocked.

"I wouldn't do it for a boy," I replied. "I would do it for me. I wouldn't have to feel like a freak anymore. I would be free from all the lies. I would be a normal person."

Shyanna started to cry. "But you would lose your beautiful tail," she said. "And what about all the wonderful things about being a mermaid? What about exploring caves, looking for long-lost treasure?

You'd never be able to talk to sea creatures again. And you would lose us."

"I would remember you," I said. "Just not all of it. And you could visit me as soon as you get your legs."

Cora was up again, swim-pacing back and forth. "You wouldn't be able to race through the sea. Or go to mermaid school or concerts. You wouldn't remember the King and Queen. You wouldn't remember the Melody Carnival. And what about your dad?"

I nodded. "I'd have to convince him to come with me. I could never leave him behind. I think he would do it. My mum was human. We could be too."

"I think this is the saddest thing I've ever heard," said Shyanna. "We would miss you."

"You haven't even started school yet," Cora said softly. "And I really wanted you to join us on the Spirit Squad," she added. "But … it's also not right for mermaids to be sad."

Shyanna lifted her head to stare at Cora. "What are you saying, Cora?"

"I don't want her to leave," Cora said. Then she turned to me and asked, "But are you really that miserable and unhappy?"

I bit my lip and twirled my hair around my finger. "I love being a mermaid. And Neptunia is so wonderful. I'd miss you two so much." I paused, thinking about how to say what I wanted to say. "It's just that ... sometimes I feel left out ... and so different from everyone else. And I'd really like to tell Owen the truth. He's always been honest with me, and he doesn't understand why I can't always be around. He was my first best friend."

"We're your best friends too," Shyanna said, her voice soft.

"I know. But Owen and I have a history. Like you two do," I explained.

"Being different isn't bad, you know," Shyanna said. "Who wants to be exactly the same as everyone else?"

She was blinking fast, and her eyes were shiny with tears.

"Stay with us," she begged. "You'd be so unhappy never being a mermaid again. We'll come to the beach with you as soon as we're thirteen. We can meet Owen when we get our legs. All of us can be friends. You can have both worlds if you stay with us. If you become human, that will be your only world."

Cora jumped up again. "We could make sure no one makes fun of you," she said.

I smiled at them. "You know I love you both. But you can't always be around to protect me."

There was a noise from the front door. Dad swam inside. "Hello! Is there a party going on in here without me?" He looked at Shyanna and Cora's faces. "Have I interrupted something? This looks like a very serious party."

I glanced at my friends and shook my head slightly, pretending to zip up my lips so they wouldn't say anything.

"Not at all, Mr Marlin!" Shyanna said. She tried to sound happy, but he frowned as if he suspected something was wrong.

"Listen, girls," he said. "The Queen wants me to let you know how thrilled she was with her concert – and you three, especially, for giving it such a good opening. She has asked the royal chef to make a special meal for us. Would you girls like to go out for dinner and then have a sleepover here with Rachel tomorrow night?"

Shyanna swam up and wrapped her arms around me tightly, hugging me like she'd never let go.

"We'd love to," Cora said, but her smile didn't last very long.

Dad frowned. He knew something was wrong.

Chapter seven

After dinner, Dad sat down with me while I was putting clam juice in my hair to make it shine. "You do want your friends to stay, don't you?" he asked. "I thought it would be nice for you, but perhaps I should have asked you first."

"Of course, Dad. It'll be great!" I ran my fingers through my hair to spread the juice around more evenly. "You know how much I love those girls. And having the Queen's chef make us dinner? Yummy!"

"I have a surprise before the girls come over," Dad said. "For the two of us. So don't make any plans."

"Okay!" I wasn't ready to have a serious talk

about becoming human yet, so I told him I was tired from all the concert excitement and went to my bedroom early that night.

I lay in bed for a long time, staring up at my ceiling. The girls were seriously making me rethink my plan. I really did love being a mermaid. I loved the sea and all the creatures, and I knew I'd miss everything I had to give up. Not only that, my dad would also have to give up the job he seemed to love so much.

The thing was, I suspected Regina was going to try to cause a lot of trouble for me. And I remembered only too well how hard it was to be made fun of all the time, especially when merkids also made fun of my mum. I missed her all the time, and I didn't care if she was part human or part penguin. I didn't want to hear anyone say horrible things about her.

If only all the mermaids could accept me for who and what I was. I had Shyanna and Cora, but

I'd always be the odd mermaid out. And what about Owen? I didn't want to lose the first best friend I'd ever had.

I finally fell asleep, these thoughts drifting through my mind.

When I woke up in the morning, Dad had already gone. I played hide-and-seek with some clown fish in the morning, and in the afternoon, I played with some dolphins who came to visit. Life in the sea really was magical. After a few more games, I made my way home. Dad would be there soon. I had no idea what his surprise would be.

"We're going on an adventure, Rach!" Dad called when he finally got home from work. "You look like you need some cheering up, and I've been working far too much. Let's go and have some fun! We both deserve it."

I nodded, trying not to look too guilty. I'd have to tell him my plans when we got home.

"I know you didn't get a big thirteen-year-old

celebration like all the other mermaids, so we're going to have our own celebration before dinner," he said, grinning. "You and I are going to sing with the whales!"

"Really?" I gasped. That had been our favourite thing to do before Mum died. We would travel outside Caspian and call to the whales. The whales didn't usually sing with other sea creatures, but they could never resist joining in when they heard Dad and me singing together. Dad had taught me how to harmonize with the whales in a special key.

We swam out of Neptunia and kept going, the two of us bouncing in and out of waves towards the deepest part of the sea. Once we were in whale territory, Dad started to sing in his glorious voice. He soon signalled for me to join him, and before I knew it, sea creatures from all depths of the sea came to watch.

We sang and sang, and dolphins and sea turtles danced around us, clapping their fins along to the music! Finally, it was time to leave. We said goodbye

to all of our new friends and began to swim back towards Neptunia. On the way back, he stopped to show me a rare frost flower growing out of the seabed.

"Is everything okay, Rachel?" Dad asked me when we got home. "I want you to be happy. If you don't like it here, we can move again."

"Oh, Dad," I said. My eyes stung, and I thought I might cry. "You love it here, don't you? Working with the Queen?"

He swam to me and put his arm around me. "The main reason we moved here was so that you would be happier. That's the most important thing to me."

I leaned against him. "I love Neptunia, Dad. I really do," I said. "And Shyanna and Cora are the best. It's just..."

"What is it?" He stared down at me with concern.

"I miss Owen. I'm afraid he's forgetting about me. I can't go and see him as much as I used to," I explained. "He was – I mean, is – my best friend. I feel like I'm losing him."

Dad nodded. He was a great listener.

"And, well, one of the mermaids found out I'm half-human," I said. "I have no idea how, but I suppose it doesn't matter. I'm afraid the teasing is going to start again. I don't know if I'll ever fit in, no matter what kingdom we go to. When mermaids find out about Mum, some of them don't like it."

His face turned red. "Who is saying these things?" he asked angrily. "I'll talk to their parents."

"No, Dad. You know that will only make it worse," I said.

He let go of me and swam in a circle, flipping his tail in frustration. "But it's not right. There has to be something we can do."

"Well," I murmured. "Perhaps there is something. I've been thinking about it a lot."

He tilted his head, waiting.

"What if we became human?" I asked softly. "I mean ... what if we went to live on land? Forever."

Chapter eight

Dad gasped. "Don't you want to be a mermaid anymore?"

"I love being a mermaid," I said. "But I've had enough of being different. If we became human together, we would eventually forget our mermaid life. We'd fit in with the humans, and I could still keep Shyanna and Rachel as friends. They could come and visit us once they got their legs. I wouldn't remember that they were mermaids, but we could still be friends. All four of us – Owen, Shyanna, Cora and me."

"Is that really what you want?" Dad asked.

I nodded. "It wouldn't be so awful, would it? I mean, you must know a lot about being human from being married to Mum."

He hugged me again. "Being different is what makes us special, Rach."

"Sometimes it's hard being special," I admitted.

Suddenly, the doorbell rang, interrupting us. Shyanna and Rachel were floating at the door. They'd arrived for the sleepover party.

"I know that." Dad sighed, looking a little bit defeated. "I'd do anything for you, Rachel. You know that. Let me see what I can do."

* * *

"Wake up, girls!"

I rubbed my eyes and looked at the clock next to my bed. It was early! Why was Dad waking us up? Didn't he know we liked to stay up as late as we could keep our eyes open for at sleepover parties?

Shyanna and Rachel were still sleeping on the floor next to my bed.

"Wakey, wakey!" Dad called.

We all groaned.

"Come on. I'll make sardine pancakes for breakfast, but you'll have to eat them quickly. In the meantime, comb your hair, brush your teeth and get ready!"

"Ready for what?" I asked, groggily. "Dad, sleepover parties don't end at seven in the morning. We still have things to do. We haven't even painted our fingernails or plaited shells into our hair."

He tried really hard without Mum, but sometimes Dad really didn't understand girl things.

"This is important," he said. "I spoke to the Queen last night."

The girls rubbed their eyes. I frowned, asking him, "Did you? When?"

"When I took the chef home last night after dinner," he explained. "I asked the Queen for a

special meeting. She's a busy lady, and the only time she could meet us is at eight o'clock this morning. So we have to get going. All of us! This is important. Lend the girls some sparkly tops and make sure you all look presentable."

Shyanna and Cora nodded – we were all excited. It wasn't often that mermaids our age got to meet the Queen in private.

"What's it about?" I asked him, glancing at my two friends, who looked equally puzzled.

"It's a secret." He wouldn't say anything else.

The girls and I jumped up out of bed and started to get ready while Dad made breakfast.

"I wonder what your dad is up to," Shyanna whispered.

I squeezed her hand. "I have no idea," I said. "All I know is that I'm sick of secrets."

Chapter nine

The King and Queen's palace was so glamorous! It was hard to believe Dad got to go there every day for work. Shyanna, Cora and I giggled when the Queen's guard announced our names outside the private quarters. We tried our hardest to stay calm when they led us into the Queen's parlour.

The Queen was sitting on her throne, wearing a light purple cloak. Her long blonde hair was plaited with sparkles and the shiniest pearls. She looked regal, elegant and completely perfect.

She stood and winked at us when we came in. "Look. It's my favourite warm-up singers and my singing teacher!" she said. The flutters in my stomach subsided. "You girls did such an amazing job at the concert. I'd like to do it again soon!"

The Queen offered us some tea, and we sat at a table in front of her throne. There were large biscuits with pink icing on a plate on the table. It might have been early, but that didn't stop Shyanna from grabbing a biscuit straight away.

"Your majesty," my dad said, bowing his head. "I asked to speak to you today about a matter of extreme importance."

We all stared at Dad.

"As you know, my daughter, Rachel, is half-human," he continued.

"I am aware," the Queen said with a smile. "Her mother – your wife – was a wonderful mermaid, wife, mother and friend. She took to our life so well. It was a pleasure to welcome her to our world with

magic. It was one of the best decisions I have ever made. I am still so sorry for your loss."

"Thank you. We are too. We miss her every day," Dad said, looking down. Then he glanced at me. "This is what I have come to discuss. The fact is that there haven't been any half-human mermaids in Neptunia for quite some time. And in the past – in other kingdoms – Rachel has been teased for being half-human."

Cora and Shyanna each grabbed one of my hands and squeezed it tightly.

The Queen frowned, but my dad kept going. "Rachel can travel to land and stay there as long as she wants. I've allowed her to explore, and while on land she has made a really special friend. A human."

The Queen nodded. "Owen," she said. "He is a good human."

My cheeks got a little warm.

"Don't look so surprised, Rachel," the Queen said. "We know about Owen. For your protection. We keep an eye on our mermaids, even when they're on land."

"Unfortunately," Dad said, "teasing is something Rachel never escapes. For that, among other reasons, she's expressed interest in becoming a human."

The Queen tilted her head and gazed at me with wide, sympathetic eyes. "Is this true?"

I nodded, unable to speak. Afraid.

"If you give up your tail, you can never get it back," the Queen said.

I swallowed, grateful the girls were holding my hands. I didn't want to think about giving up being a mermaid forever, but it seemed like the only solution. I wanted Owen to be a part of my life all the time. I wanted to have a normal life.

"I have another idea," my dad said. "One that might make Rachel reconsider her choice."

We all stared at him. Even the Queen.

"What if we grant Owen temporary merman status to visit Rachel? He's thirteen, so he could do the same as mermaids do on land, only in reverse. A few hours in the sea to see Rachel's life. And then Rachel could share her friends and her world here with Owen. She wouldn't have to keep her real self a secret from him anymore."

"Exposure to humans is always risky," the Queen said, frowning.

"But my mum proved to be trustworthy!" I cried.

She raised her hand. "Let me finish, please."

I pressed my lips tightly.

"Owen has the right human qualities to be trusted," the Queen continued. "The question is, would having Owen visit you here stop you wanting to turn to human form permanently?"

I nodded my head vigorously. If Owen knew the truth about my life, that would really help. My dad was a genius.

"He would have to keep the secret," the Queen said. "And if he didn't, he would turn into a merman. He would never be able to return to human form. His family would believe he was lost at sea. This is a delicate matter that must be taken very seriously. Do you understand what you are asking?"

I thought about Owen and how he always said there was nothing that could prevent him from being my friend. I knew he could be trusted. I nodded again.

"I do, and I know they are only teenagers," my dad said. "But I believe they have old souls and can be trusted. Their friendship is stronger than any I've ever witnessed."

The Queen sipped her tea and then put down her cup. "From what I've seen, I agree with your assessment. Their bond is incredible."

"Sometimes a strong friendship can be as strong as love," my dad said. "Wouldn't you agree, Queen?"

"I would indeed," she said with a smile. "Rachel, you may tell Owen the truth. He can be brought here if he agrees. It is his choice. If he doesn't agree, he will forget what you've told him."

"Really?" I whispered. I was in shock.

"Once you tell him," the Queen explained, "you must be aware that if he chooses not to be part merman, you will no longer be allowed to visit him.

Too much exposure after that may wear off the mermaid magic, and he could eventually remember the truth about you. That cannot be allowed to happen."

I loved being a mermaid far too much to give it up. I knew in my heart that being different didn't mean being bad. If I could tell my best friend the truth and bring him to Neptunia to see my life here, it would be worth all the hassle. I was sure he wouldn't turn me down. I was so sure, I was willing to risk losing him forever.

I would tell Owen the truth and offer him a chance to see a life that other humans couldn't even imagine. The world beneath the sea. Having the four of us together would be a dream come true. Owen, Shyanna, Cora and me!

I gulped and nodded at the Queen. She snapped her finger, and a mermaid appeared and gave me a magic tablet. It would turn Owen into a merman.

If he chose to be one.

Chapter ten

The next morning, Shyanna, Cora and my dad each hugged me before I left to find Owen. I was so nervous. I couldn't believe this was really happening! It felt like a dream.

I found Owen on the beach in our special spot. I had sent Owen a message the night before, so I knew he'd be waiting for me. I didn't know how to tell him my secret, so I just blurted it out. When I had finished telling him the truth, and the rules about knowing the truth and the choice he had to make, he didn't look upset at all. He didn't even look that surprised. I suppose that is a normal boy response to most things.

"Mermaids," he said, smiling. "That's the most amazing thing I've ever heard."

"You aren't cross or freaked out?" I asked.

"It's a bit strange, but I always knew there was something different about you. Not strange different, but magical different."

"Did you?" I asked.

"I think that's what brought us together. And of course I can keep it a secret. You're my best friend. And of course I want to see your world!"

My cheeks glowed with happiness. He looked back at me, and I saw that his cheeks were glowing too. He touched his neck, and I noticed he was wearing the shark tooth necklace I had made him for his birthday. I touched the shell necklace he gave me, the one that I never took off.

For a moment I wondered if we'd ever be more

than friends, but then I tucked that idea away. I didn't want to ruin what we had right now.

"Merpeople," he said as we walked towards the sea. "I always wondered why you were constantly on the beach, but you would never swim." He pointed at my legs. "I can't wait to see your tail!"

"I can't wait to see yours!" I said, and we both stared down at his legs.

"Me neither!" he yelled, and then he started to run towards the water.

"Wait!" I called and laughed.

"You have to take this first," I said as I pulled out the magic tablet the Queen had given me. "Are you sure about all of this? You don't need to think about it for a bit longer or anything?"

He nodded. "Are you mad? I can't wait!"

"Okay. Then take this, and we'll go to Neptunia to meet my friends," I said.

He swallowed the tablet. "Tastes like fish," he said, smiling. He stared down at his legs, waiting.

I laughed and pulled him into the sea. My tail spread out, shimmering in the sunshine.

"Wow!" he said, his eyes sparkling in amazement.

And then we both watched as his tail spread out until his legs disappeared and a tail took their place. It was a glorious tail, reds and oranges twinkling in the water. He beamed at me, and then we dove down under a wave. The grin didn't leave his face. He was an amazing swimmer and took to his fins straight away.

Owen was like a little boy, stopping to admire every shellfish and jellyfish and waving lobster. He played with the dolphins that came to greet us, and the grumpy old whale that swam by and blew a spout of water made him laugh.

When we finally arrived at Neptunia, Shyanna and Cora were waiting in Walrus Waterpark for us. They looked as happy as me and Owen. The girls hugged Owen like he was an old friend. And it was then that I knew that this was the right decision.

But soon, we weren't the only merpeople at Walrus Waterpark. Regina and a group of her mermaid friends arrived.

"Who is this?" Regina asked, swimming closer.

"I'm Owen," he said, not intimidated. "And this is my best friend, Rachel, and my new friends Shyanna and Cora. We're merpeople!"

We all laughed at his enthusiasm.

"I know what we are," Regina said, turning her nose up a bit. But he also intrigued her, I could tell. "Where did you come from?"

He winked at her. "That's a secret between friends. Do you mind?" he asked, and then he twirled up and did a double flip turn. "I have to say, I like Neptunia a lot. You'd better get used to seeing me around."

Regina was not smiling. I had a feeling I was going to have to put up with her a lot once school started, but I didn't care. Having Owen here was more important than worrying about Regina.

She swam away, with her friends following behind. I grabbed Owen's hand. His time was almost up, and we had to get him back to land. "Come on, Owen, we have to go," I said.

"We're so pleased we've been able to meet you!" Shyanna said.

"And we'll come and visit you on land as soon as we're thirteen and get our legs!" Cora added.

We were all so happy to add a fourth best friend to our friendship circle. "Come on, Owen," I called. "Let's get back to the beach. You can come back and visit soon!"

"Just try to keep me away," he said.

Legend of mermaids

These creatures of the sea have many secrets. Although people have believed in mermaids for centuries, nobody has ever proven their existence. People all over the world are attracted to mysterious mermaids.

The earliest mermaid story dates back to around 1000 BC in an Assyrian legend. A goddess loved a human man but killed him accidentally. She fled to the water in shame. She tried to change into a fish, but the water would not let her hide her true nature. She lived the rest of her days as half-woman, half-fish.

Later, the ancient Greeks whispered tales of fishy women called sirens. These beautiful but deadly beings lured sailors to their graves. Many sailors feared or respected mermaids because of their association with doom.

Note: This text was taken from *The Girl's Guide to Mermaids: Everything Alluring about These Mythical Beauties* by Sheri A. Johnson (Capstone Press, 2012).

Talk about it

1. Before Rachel moved to Neptunia, she was teased at school. Teasing is a type of bullying, and bullying is never right. Can you describe a time when you felt bullied? How did it make you feel? What did you do?

2. Were you surprised by Cora's reaction when she found out Rachel's secret? What about Owen's reaction? How do you think you would have reacted?

3. Friendship is a special type of love. What qualities make good friendships? How are those qualities shown in this story?

4. What would you have done if you were Owen? Would you have said yes to Rachel's request so quickly?

Write it down

1. Pretend you are Rachel. Write a "for" and "against" list to support your decision to tell Owen your big secret.

2. Rachel misses her mum. Write a letter to an important person in your life. You can choose to give it to them or to keep it to yourself.

3. Rachel was half-human, which made her different. Our differences are what make us unique. Write a paragraph about your unique qualities and how they make you special.

4. Write an alternate ending for the story. Perhaps Owen says no to Rachel's request, or Regina follows Rachel and tells everyone her secret. It's your ending, so you can finish the story in whatever way you think best.

About the author

Janet Gurtler has written many well-received books for the Young Adult market. Mermaid Kingdom is her first series for younger readers. She lives near the Canadian Rockies in Calgary, Canada, with her husband, son and a chubby Chihuahua called Bruce.

About the illustrator

Katie Wood fell in love with drawing
when she was very young. Since graduating
from Loughborough University School
of Art and Design in 2004, she has been
living her dream working as a freelance
illustrator. From her studio in Leicester,
she creates bright and lively illustrations
for books and magazines all over the world.